OLD TURTLE'S SOCCER TEAM

**Written and illustrated
by Leonard Kessler**

A Young Yearling Book

Published by
Dell Publishing
a division of
Bantam Doubleday Dell Publishing Group, Inc.
666 Fifth Avenue
New York, New York 10103

SPECIAL THANKS FROM
OLD TURTLE TO:
Glenn Nelson, soccer coach
Helen Bernstein, soccer coach
Carl Orletti
Ethel Kessler

ISBN: 0-440-40285-9

Reprinted by arrangement with William Morrow & Company, Inc.,
on behalf of Greenwillow Books

Printed in the United States of America

April 1990

10 9 8 7 6 5 4 3 2 1

W

CONTENTS

1. Who Wants to Play Soccer?

"Look at my birthday present,"
said Cat.

"A soccer ball!" said Rabbit.

"Who knows how to play soccer?"
asked Frog.

"What?" Duck asked.

"SOCCER!" Frog shouted.

P O W !

Duck hit Rabbit.

"Why did you hit Rabbit?"

asked Frog.

"You said SOCK HER,"

Duck answered.

"No, silly. I said SOCCER.

It's a game," said Frog.

"I know how to play soccer,"
  said Old Turtle.

"We can have a soccer team."

"I have the ball," said Cat.

"Hurrah for Cat and Turtle,"
  Goose cheered.

"Hurrah for SOCCER!" Chicken shouted.

"What?" asked Duck.

"SOCCER!" they shouted.

Duck socked Rabbit again.

"That is not funny.

You can't play on our team

if you hit Rabbit," said Old Turtle.

"Who wants to play

on your old team anyway?"

Duck said.

She went off into the woods.

"Let's play soccer," said Goose.

They ran to the soccer field.

Big Raccoon and his friends

were there.

They were kicking a soccer ball.

"We are the Rockets.

What is the name of your team?"

Little Raccoon asked.

"We don't have a name," Frog answered.

"They are the No-Names,"

said Big Raccoon.

Little Raccoon giggled.

"Do you want to play?" he asked.

"Our team is not ready
 to play yet," said Old Turtle.

"Yes we are. Let's play," said Goose.

"Yeh team!" shouted Cat.

Little Raccoon kicked the ball.

"I have it!" called Chicken.

"No. No. You don't catch the ball,"
the Rockets shouted.

"Only the goalie can catch the ball,"
said Big Raccoon.

"Let's play," said Cat.

He tackled Little Raccoon.

"No. No. This is not a

football game," Big Raccoon yelled.

"Here's the ball," Big Raccoon said.

"Let me kick it," said Frog.

"Let me," said Chicken.

"No. Let me kick the ball,"

shouted Goose.

C R A S H !

They all fell down.

Big Raccoon picked up the ball.
"They don't know
how to play soccer," he said.
The Rockets walked off the field.

2. Learning the Rules

"If you really want to play soccer,
you'll have to learn the rules,"
Old Turtle said.
They all nodded their heads.

Rules

Each team has a goal.
The goalie protects the <u>goal</u>.
His shirt is a different color
than the other players.

GOAL ← GOALIE   GOALIE → GOAL

He is the only player who can catch,
throw, or pick up the ball.

If one team gets the ball into
the other team's goal, that team
gets one point. They made a <u>goal</u>!

GOAL

The team with the most points wins!

"I want to learn how to kick
the ball," said Goose.
"You will learn how to kick,"
said Old Turtle.
"You will also learn how
to hit the ball
with your head,
your chest,
your belly,
your legs,
and your feet."

"HEAD, CHEST, BELLY, LEGS, FEET.
WOW!" said Frog.

"But remember, only the goalie
can catch, throw, or pick up the ball,"
said Old Turtle.

Duck came out of the woods.
She tiptoed up to the field.
She hid behind a tree.
She watched her friends
kicking the ball.
"They don't want me on their team."

Duck kicked a pile of leaves.

"Some friends," she said.

She kicked an old paper bag.

The soccer ball rolled near Duck.

She kicked the ball hard.

WHAM!

The ball went over Dog's head
into the goal.

"Who kicked that ball?"
asked Old Turtle.

"I did," said Duck.
"You are a good kicker,"
said Dog.

"You may play on our team,

but no more hitting,"

said Old Turtle.

"No more hitting," Duck said.

"Shake," said Rabbit.

"Shake," said Duck.

3. **Practice, Practice**

Every day the players met
at the soccer field.
Old Turtle blew his whistle.
"Practice time," he called.
"First we will run."

"Now we will kick."

"Always aim at something when you kick."

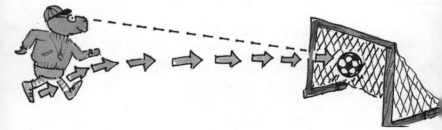

"Time to dribble."

ROLL THE BALL ALONG THE GROUND WITH YOUR FEET, WHILE YOU ARE RUNNING.

"Use your head two ways."

TO THINK

AND TO PUNCH THE BALL WITH YOUR HEAD. THAT'S CALLED HEADING.

"And pass the ball with your

HEAD, CHEST, BELLY, LEGS, FEET."

WOW

For the next week
they practiced kicking,
dribbling, passing,
and heading.

"Good teamwork,"
Old Turtle called.
"Now we are ready
to play the Rockets."

Old Turtle opened a big box.

"Here are your shirts," he said.

"**O. T. S. T.**"

"What does it mean?" asked Rabbit.

"Old Turtle's Soccer Team,"
said Old Turtle.

4. O. T. S. T. is Ready

"Here comes the No-Name team,"
said Big Raccoon.
"We have a name now.
Look at our shirts," said Frog.
"We are Old Turtle's Soccer Team,"
said Rabbit.

"But did you learn

how to play soccer?"

asked Little Raccoon.

"Let's play a game.

Then you will find out," said Cat.

Old Turtle kicked the ball.

W H O M P.

The game began.

The Rockets ran and kicked.
Little Raccoon kicked the ball
at the goal.
"I have it," said Dog.
He caught the ball.
"Nice playing," shouted Frog.

Dog tossed the ball.

Little Raccoon stopped the ball

with his foot.

"Look out, Dog!" Old Turtle shouted.

But it was too late.

Little Raccoon kicked the ball

into the goal.

"One point for the Rockets,"

called the referee.

"Come on, team. We can tie
the score," Cat said.
Frog kicked the ball
to Old Turtle.
He passed the ball to Duck.
She kicked it to Rabbit.

W H O M P.

Rabbit punched the ball
with her head.

"Good shot," called Old Turtle.

"One point for our team."

"We have a tie game," said Cat.

Duck dribbled the ball
down the field.
Little Raccoon stepped
on Duck's foot.
"Ouch!" Duck yelled.
She fell down.
"I'm sorry," said Little Raccoon.

"Duck is hurt," Chicken said.

"Do you think you can play?"
asked Old Turtle.

"I will try," said Duck.

"We need you," said Rabbit.

"Halftime," called the referee.

Duck limped off the field.

"Rest your foot," Old Turtle said.

He put a bandage on Duck's foot.

5. Sock It to Them

"Second half," called the referee.

"OK team," said Old Turtle.

"Sock it to them."

W H O M P !

Big Raccoon kicked the ball

into the air.

Duck ran to get it.

"Stop the game!" called Frog.

"The ball is stuck
 on Duck's beak."

"Pull the ball off," said Chicken.

P O O O O O O O O O O F.

All the air

went out of the ball.

"Toss in a new ball,"
  the referee called.
"I have a sore beak
  and a sore foot," said Duck.
"But you are not a sorehead,"
  said Rabbit.
  She hugged Duck.

The referee looked at her watch.

"Two minutes to play.

The score is one-all," she called.

The Rockets kicked the ball.

Cat stopped it with his foot.

He kicked the ball to Rabbit.

"Go, Rabbit, go!" shouted Old Turtle.

Rabbit dribbled the ball
past the Rockets.
"Get that ball,"
Little Raccoon yelled.
"Pass the ball,"
called Old Turtle.

"Pass the ball to me,"
Duck shouted.
Rabbit kicked the ball to Duck.
"Duck has a sore foot.
She can't kick,"
yelled Big Raccoon.

Duck took aim.

WHOMP!

The ball zoomed past
Big Raccoon into the goal.
"The game is over.
We won! We won!"
Frog cheered.

"Duck, how did you kick
that winning goal?
You have a sore right foot,"
said Little Raccoon.

"Yes," said Duck.
"But I can also kick
with my left foot!"
PLOMP.
She kicked the ball
with her left foot.

"Your team played very well,"
said Big Raccoon.
"Not bad for a No-Name team,"
said Old Turtle.
"We are not a No-Name team,"
said Frog.

"We are
OLD TURTLE'S SOCCER TEAM!"
They all cheered.

Many of Leonard Kessler's favorite books are about sports. He has written stories about baseball, football, track-and-field, marathon running, and winter games.

Over the years he has received letters from his readers asking, "When are you going to write a book about soccer?" So he asked his friend Old Turtle to help him write a soccer book. On his studio shelf, along with his running shoes, sneakers, baseball mitt, bat, and ball, there is now a soccer ball.